AF257961

My Worldwide Amateur Radio Friends

Rob Norman

My Ham Radio Friends

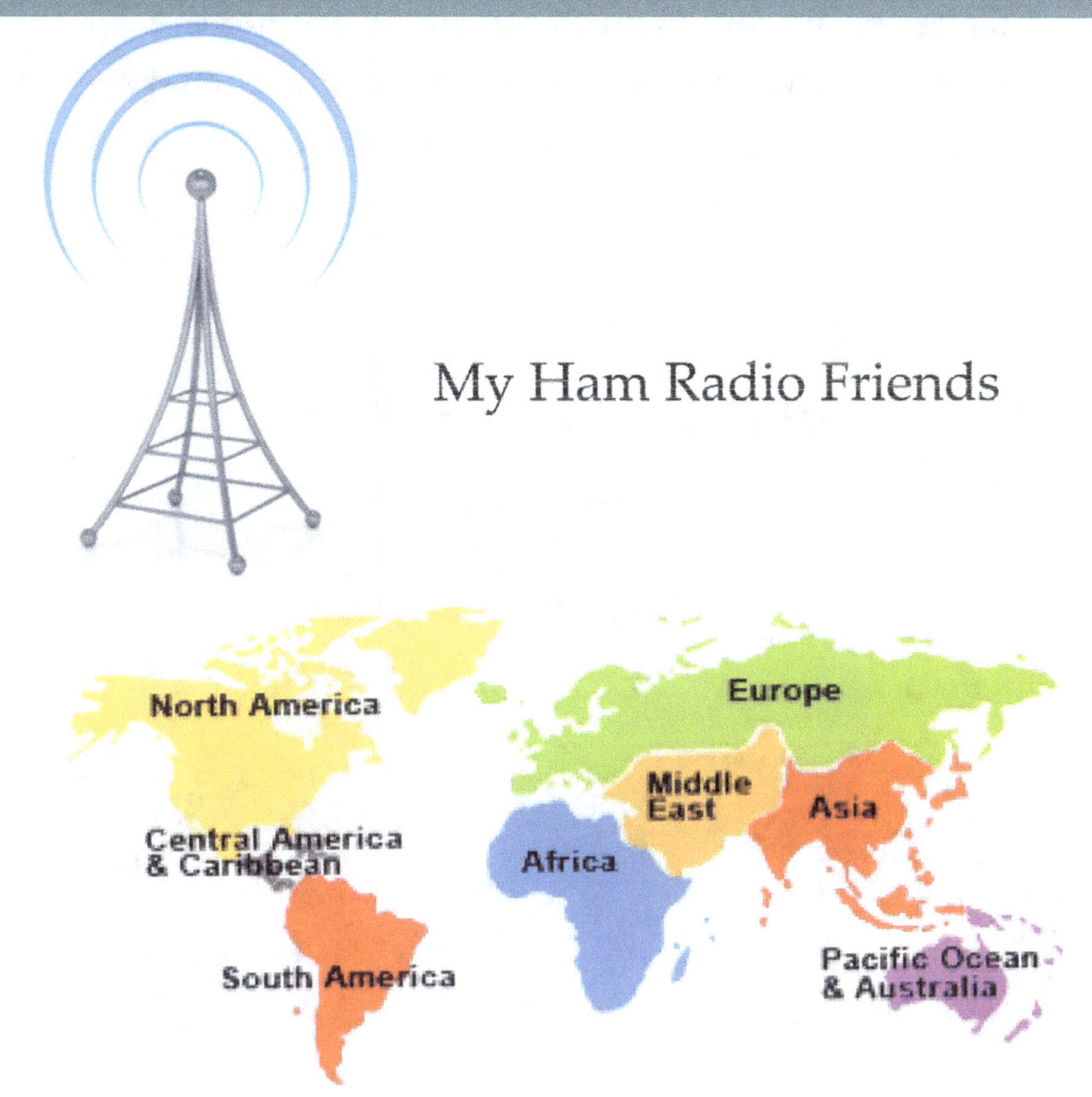

This book was originally published as a Kindle ebook. Whether You are using the Kindle or Paperback format, I hope this book gives You Information, Inspiration and Enjoyment.

Rob, VK5SW. www.VK5SW.com

Since certain radio waves can travel around the earth, Amateur Radio operators are able to make friends in various countries of the world.

Your Ham Radio Friends

AVA in France.

ELKE in England.

TIM in the U.S.A.

GRACE in Italy.

TOMMY in Hawaii.

YIPING in China.

My Worldwide Amateur Radio Friends

Amateur Radios

Amateur Radio Antennas

 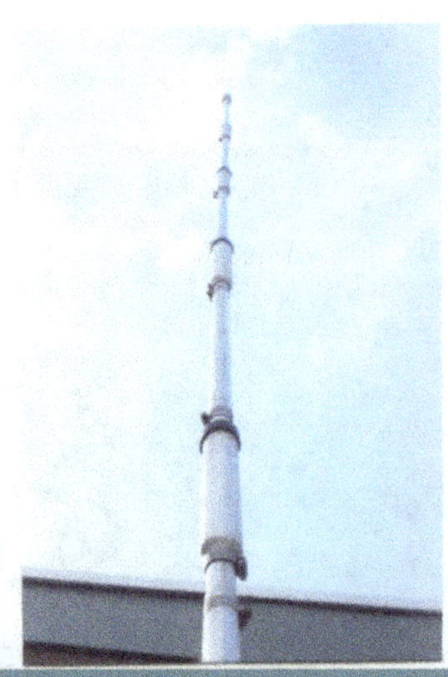 

Introduction

The hobby of Amateur Radio, also known as 'Ham Radio' has been around for well over 100 years.

It basically involves qualified people communicating with each other using amateur radios. Today, there are about three million licensed amateur radio operators throughout the world. Amateur Radio stations consist of specialist radios called amateur radios and outdoor antennas which receive and radiate the radio signals. Since certain radio waves can travel around the world, amateur radio operators are able to communicate with each other worldwide and make friends around the globe.

This interactive ebook has been written to introduce you to the hobby and give you some idea of what it is like to chat to other children in various countries of the world using a pretend microphone. Many different forms of communicating are used by Amateurs. Speaking into a microphone is just one of them. Ham Radio is enjoyed by all ages, from the young to the elderly. Hams come from all walks of life.

I hope you have fun with this ebook and that it sparks your interest in this rewarding and exciting hobby.

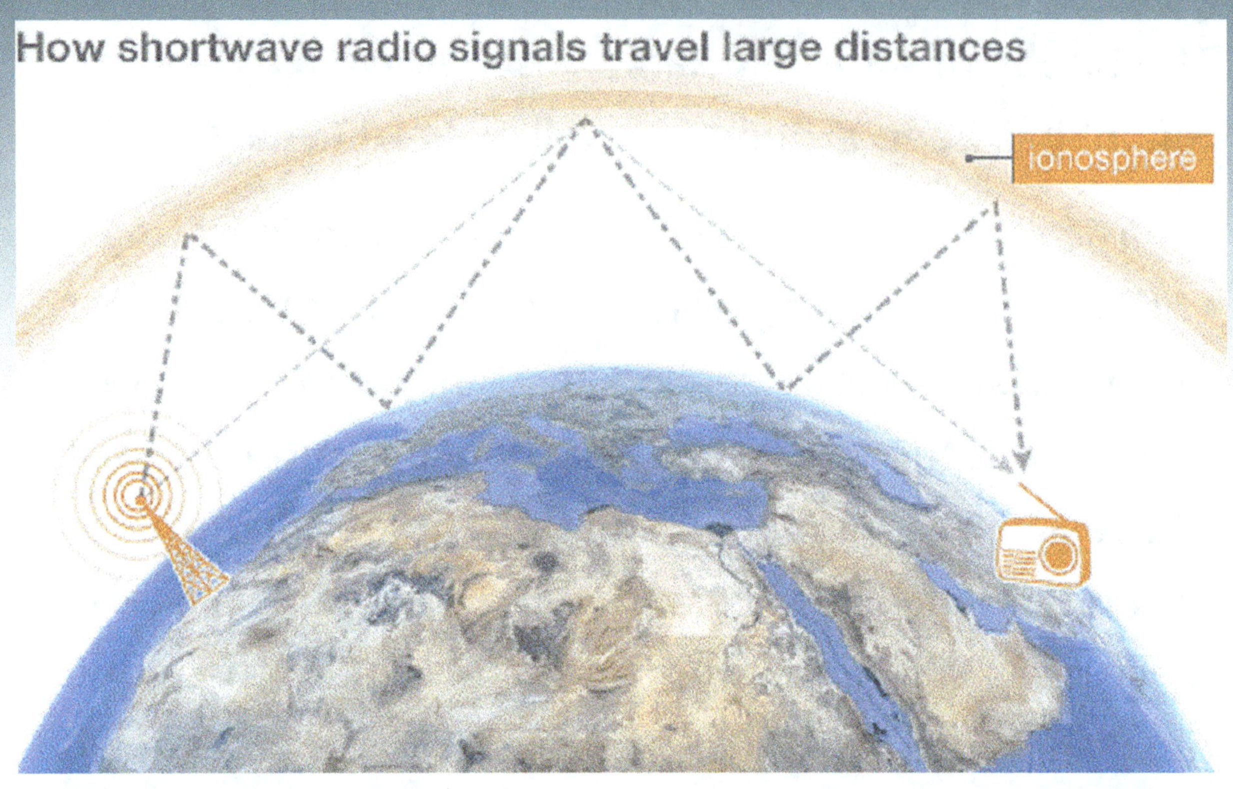

How shortwave radio signals travel large distances
ionosphere

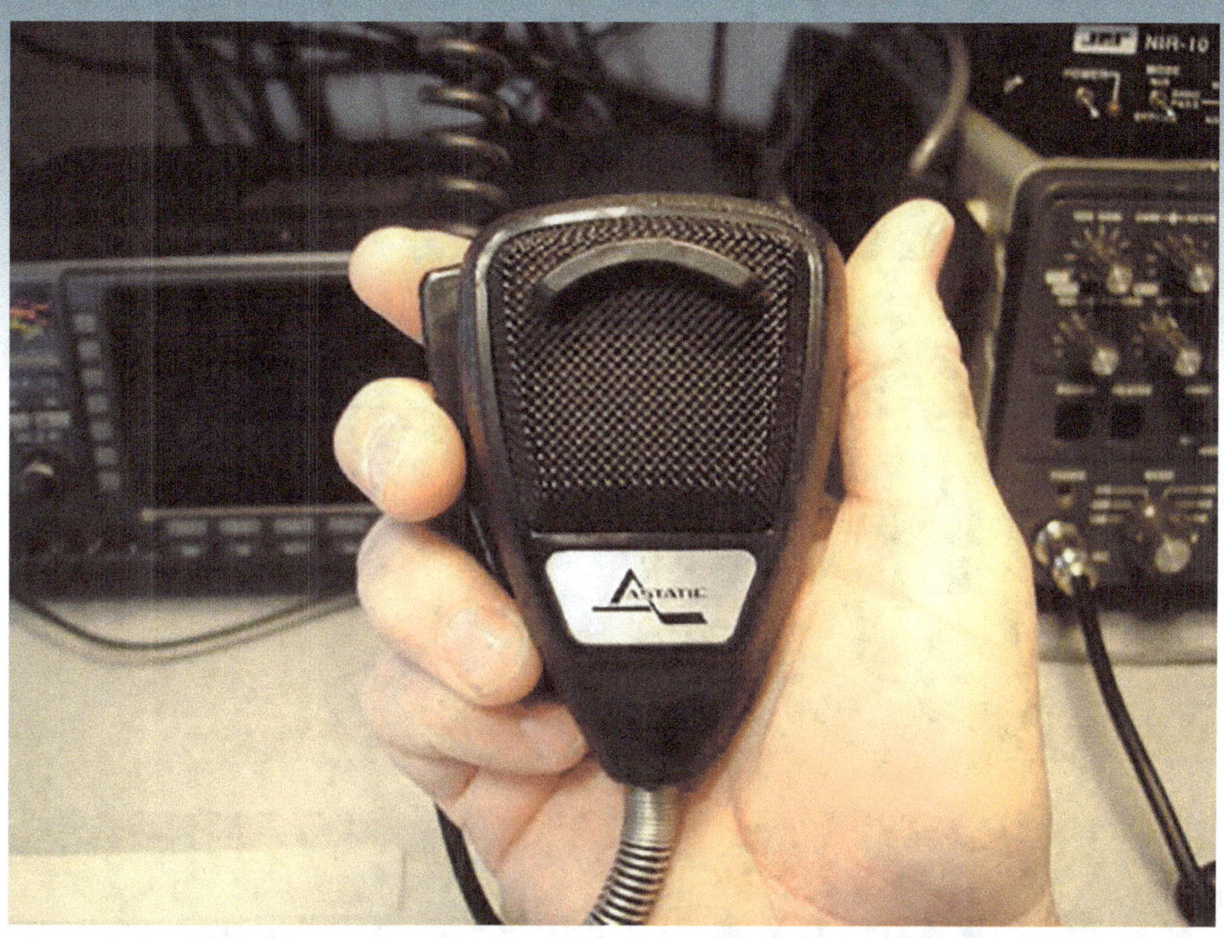

Amateur Radio - Worldwide Radio Communication

This is your Amateur Radio Station.

From here, using your microphone,

you can talk to people all over

The World.

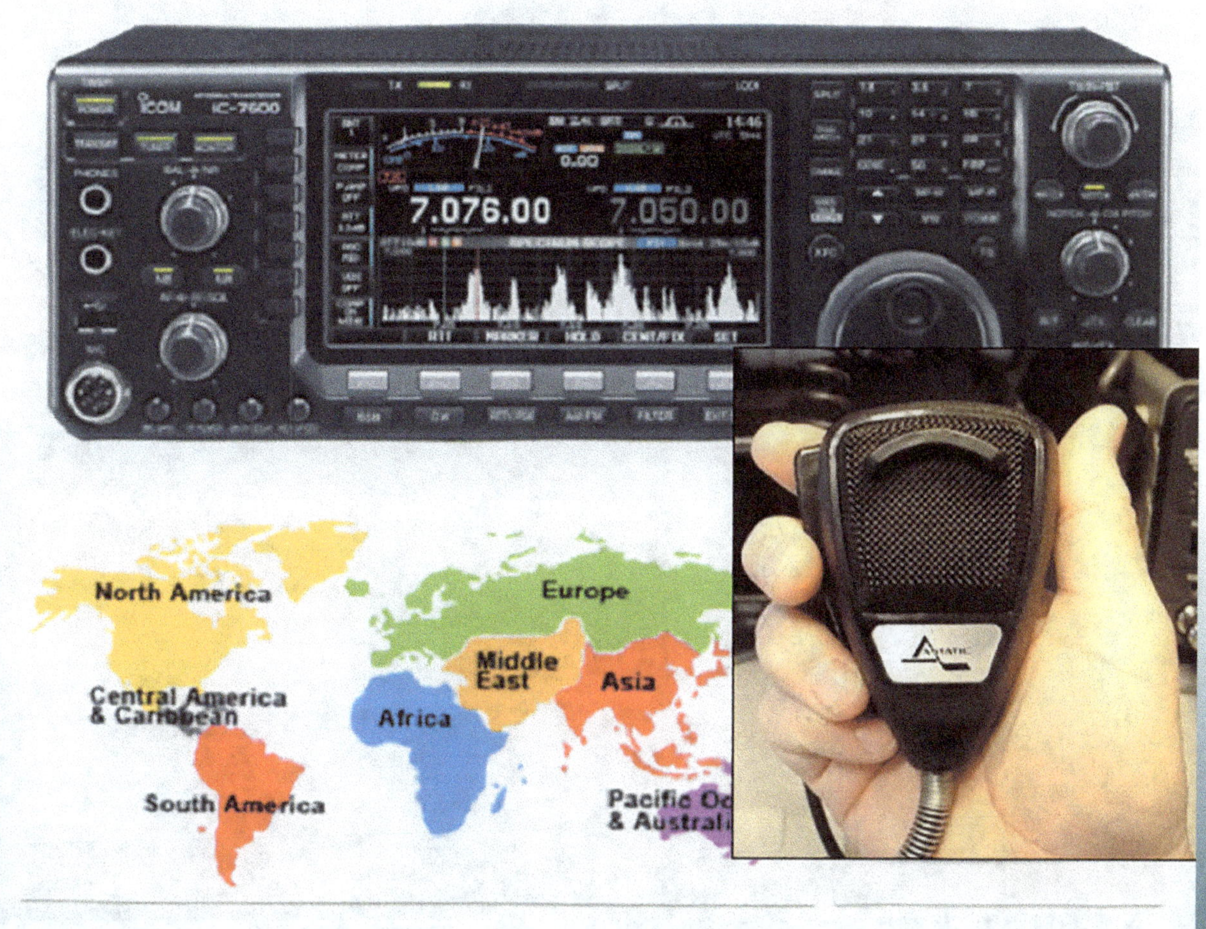

This is Amateur Radio operator ' AVA '.

Ava is 11 years old and lives in

FRANCE. (Europe)

Pick up your pretend microphone, speak into it and tell Ava your name, age and where you live.

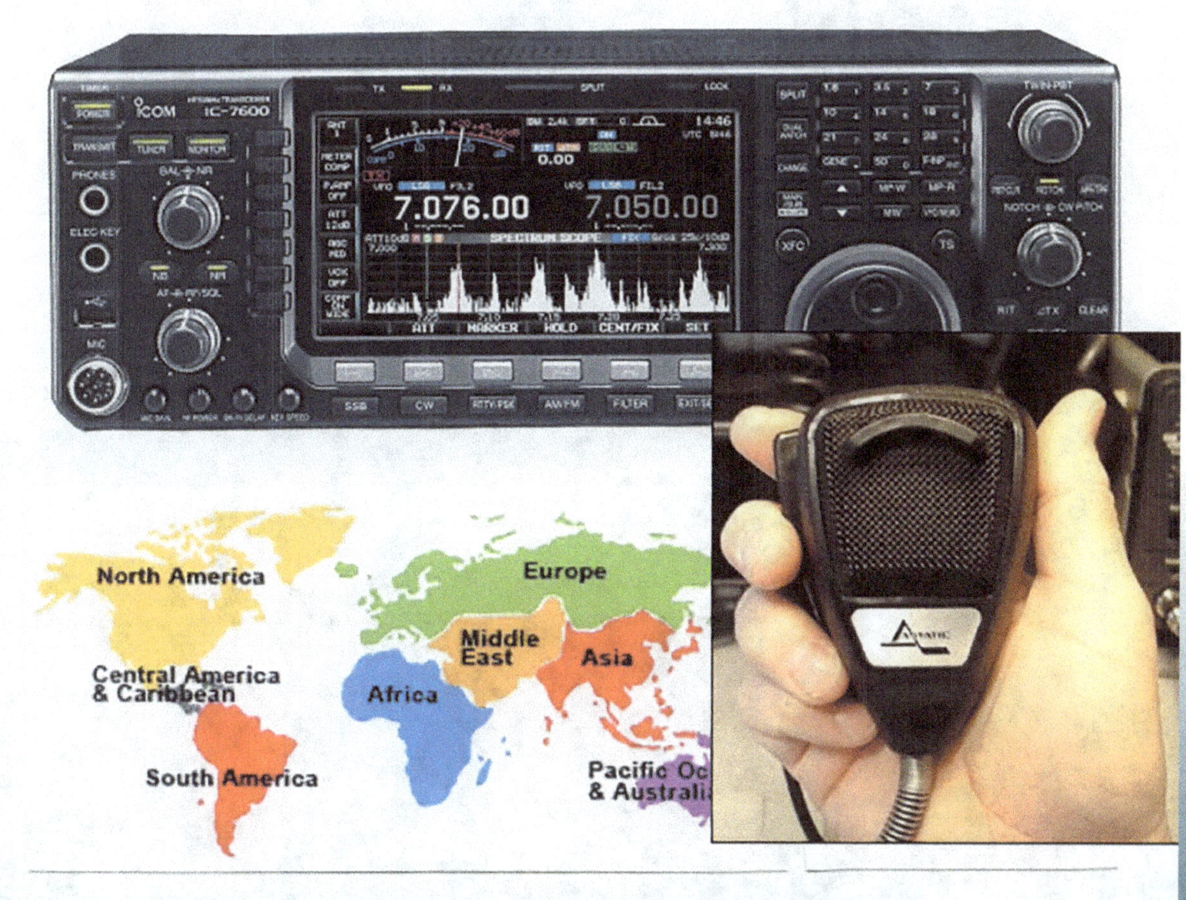

This is Amateur Radio operator ' TIM '.

Tim is 8 years old and lives in the

U.S.A.. (North America)

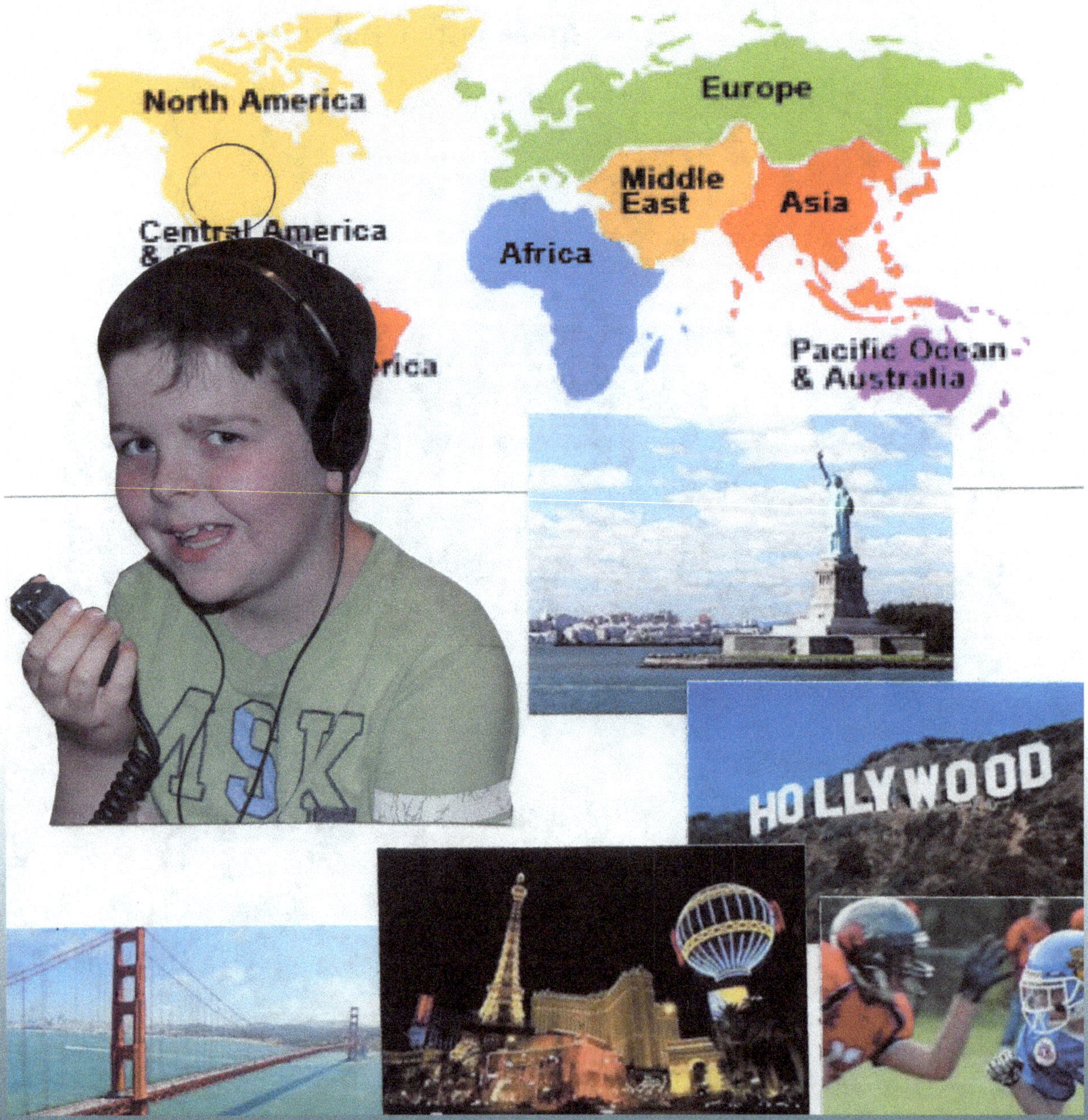

Using your pretend microphone, speak

into it and tell Tim about your family.

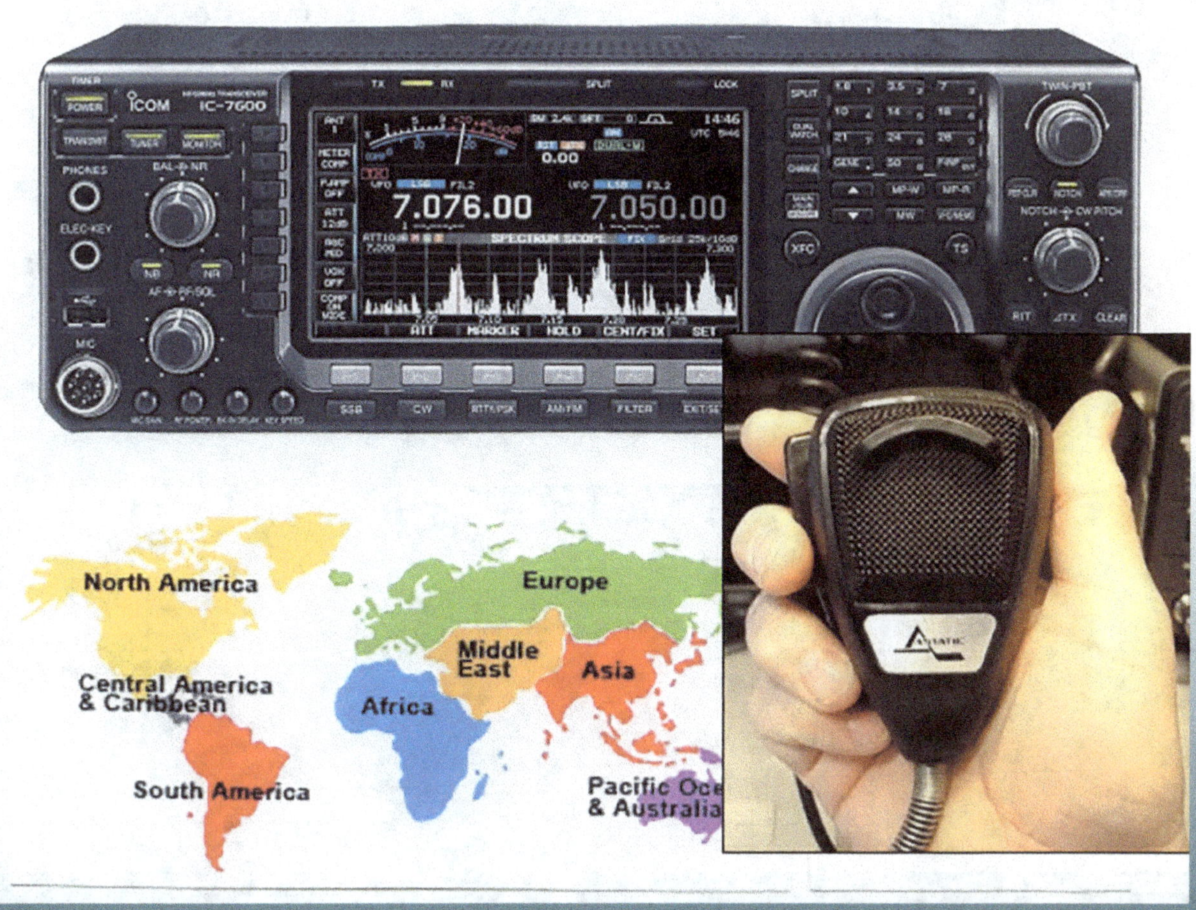

Amateur Radio operator ' TOMMY '

is 9 years old and lives in

HAWAII.

Using your pretend microphone, tell

Tommy what you like to do most of all.

This is Amateur Radio operator ' ELKE '.

Elke is 14 years old and lives in

ENGLAND. (Europe)

Using your pretend microphone, tell

Elke what types of sport you like to play.

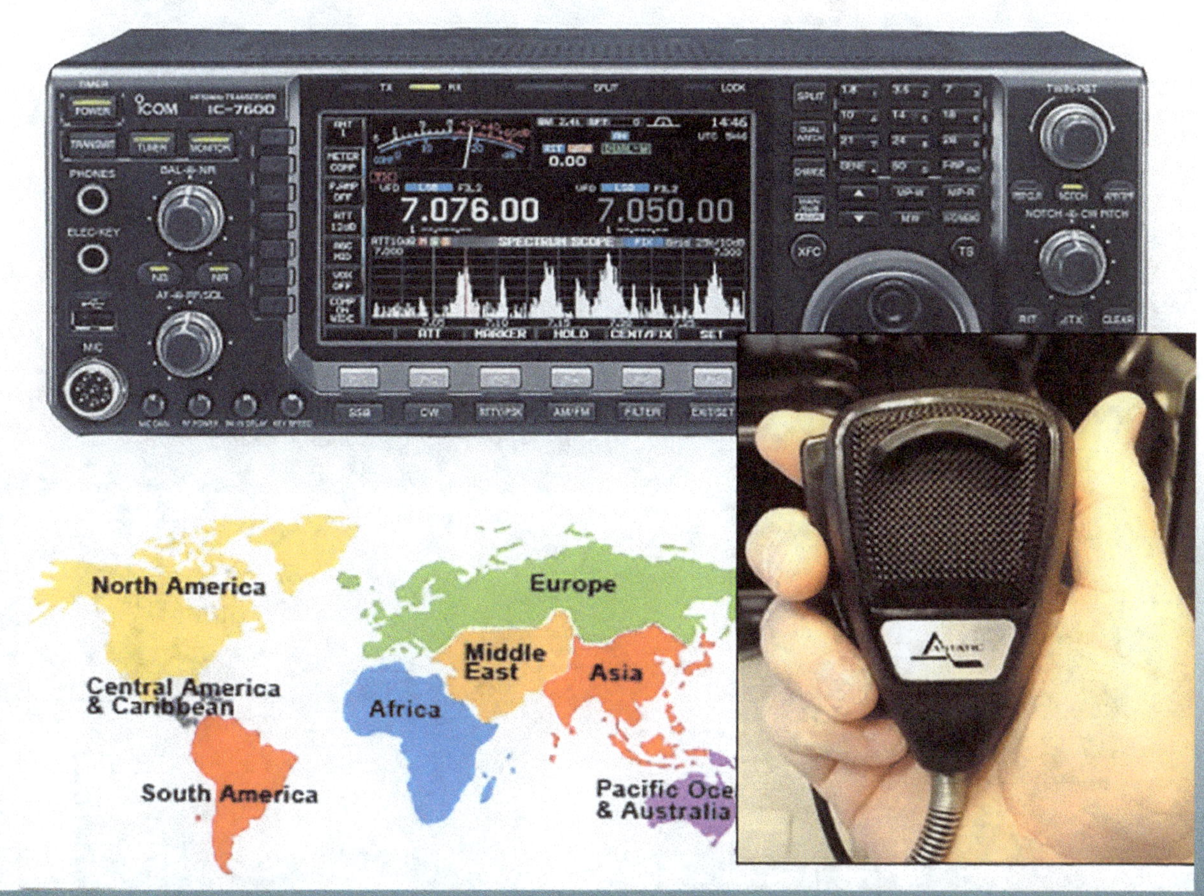

Amateur Radio operator ' YIPING '

is 12 years old and lives in

CHINA. (Asia)

Using your microphone, tell Yiping

about the books you have read recently.

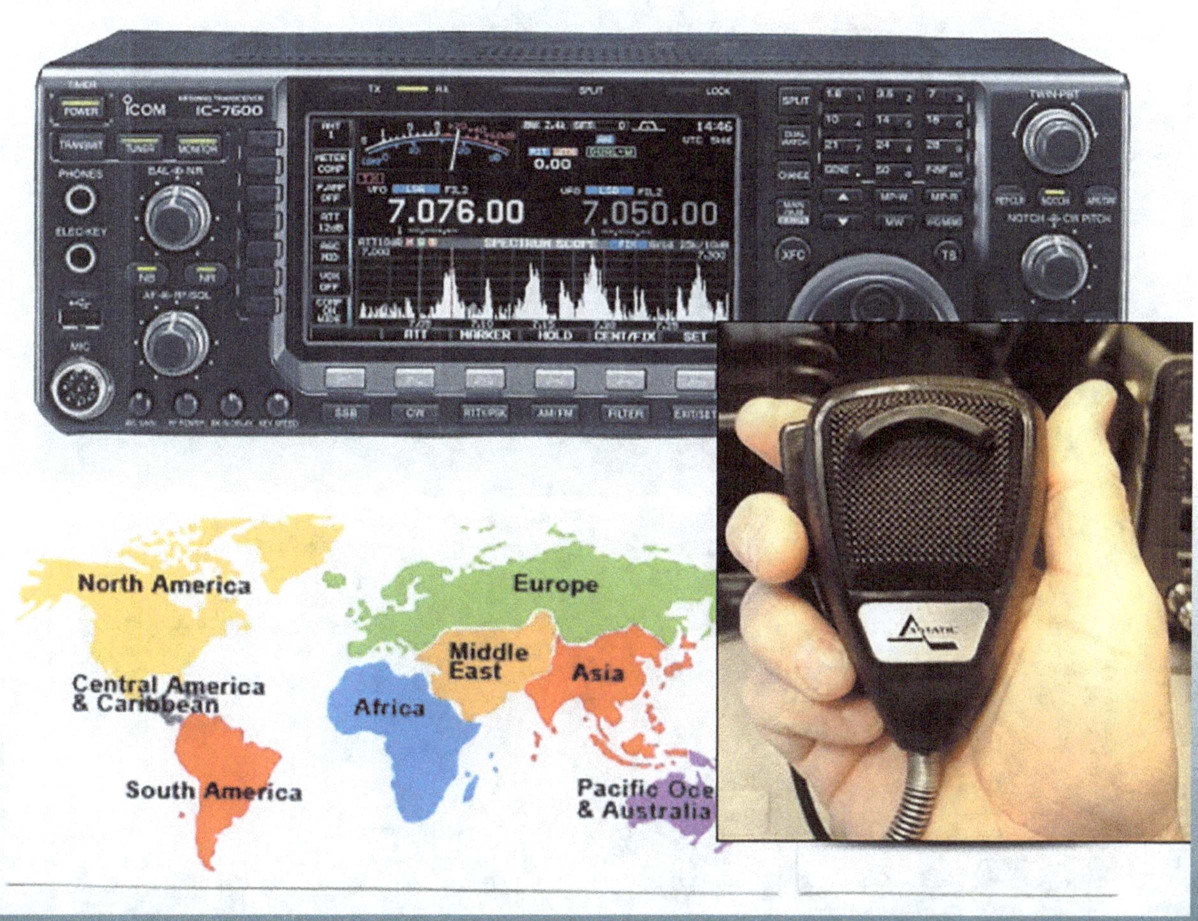

This is Amateur Radio operator ' GRACE '.

Grace is 8 years old and lives in

ITALY. (Europe)

Using your microphone,

tell Grace about your other

hobbies, apart from Amateur Radio.

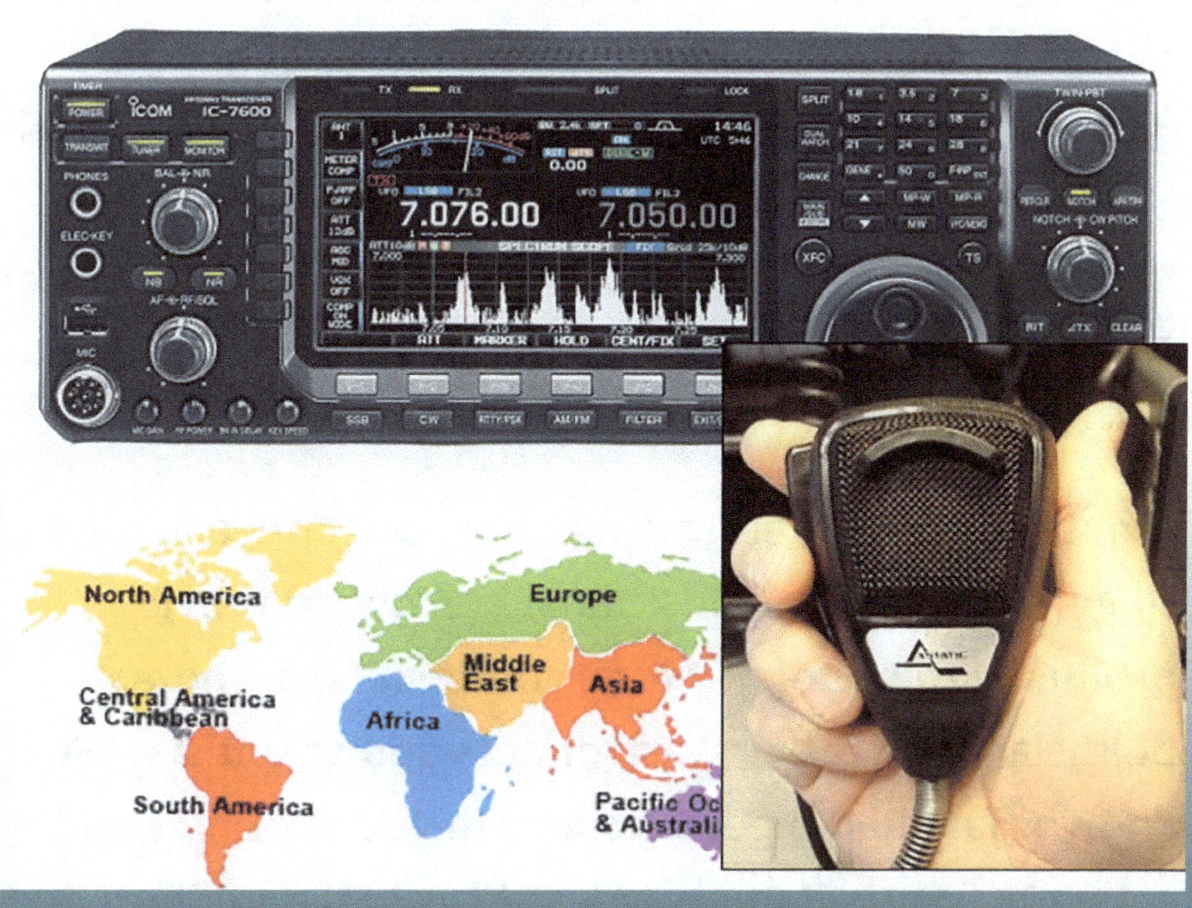

Communicating around the world has never been easier. The Internet has revolutionised this, but Amateur Radio is unique in its ability to be a reliable form of communication no matter the natural disaster that may befall us. It may be bush fires in Australia, earthquakes in South America, floods in England or tornados in the US. Ham Radio still gets through.

Millions of people around the globe find this hobby to be a stimulating pastime which rewards them with much enjoyment and friendships. It often leads people to employment in electronics and associated industries. Amateur Radio clubs are widespread and enable likeminded people to share their common interest. Examinations can be taken here by all ages to obtain an amateur radio license. Each licensed Ham Radio operator is given a callsign to identify him or her. This callsign also indicates the country in which they live.

Amateur Radio operators include nobel prize winners, singer/songwriters, musicians, hollywood movie producers/directors, actors, composers, authors, politicians, professors, astronauts and scientists. Well known Ham Radio personalities include country and western singers Patty Loveless KD4WUJ and Chet

Atkins W4CGP sk, singer Donnie Osmond WD4SKT, The Eagles band member Joe Walsh WB6ACU, newsreader Walter Cronkite KB2GSD sk, actor Marlon Brando FO5GJ sk, Priscilla Presley NY6YOS, King Hussein of Jordan JY1 sk and Dick Smith VK2DIK.

Ham Radio is enjoyed by all kinds of people.

If this ebook has sparked your interest in this hobby, I encourage you to take the first step towards a rewarding past time and google 'Amateur Radio Association' or similar in your country or city. This can lead you to a hobby which enables you to make friends around the world and change your life for the better.

Here are the website addresses of a few Amateur Radio Organizations but there are many more through out the world.

North America -   www.arrl.org

England   -   www.rsgb.org

Australia   -   www.wia.org.au

Japan   -   www.jarl.org

South Africa   -   www.sarl.org.za

Since certain radio waves can travel around the earth, Amateur Radio operators are able to make friends in various countries of the world.

Your Ham Radio Friends

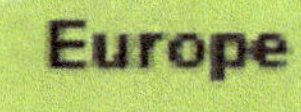

<u>AVA</u> in France.	<u>ELKE</u> in England.
<u>TIM</u> in the U.S.A.	<u>GRACE</u> in Italy.
<u>TOMMY</u> in Hawaii.	<u>YIPING</u> in China.

Amateur Radio Friends around the World share the capability of communicating via Radio Waves.

Come back soon and say Hello to Your Amateur Radio Friends. Ask them how they are going and tell them what You have been doing. They would love to hear from You.

Since Covid hit, 'Eric, 4Z1UG' and Amateur Friends have created 'A Virtual Ham Radio Expo' experience online which is held twice a year at present. Presentations are given here by Amateurs demonstrating various aspects of the Hobby. Possibly 60 or more presentations highlight the individual Operator's passion within Amateur Radio. The interactivity of this event is really excellent and highly recommended.

https://www.qsotodayhamexpo.com/

G'Day

Australia, Down Under. Land of the Kangaroo.

Rob Norman VK5SW
www.VK5SW.com
An Australian Interactive Amateur Radio Website

150 Videos and Music Slideshows which Rob has created.
Search ' vk5sw ' on You tube, Using Your Smart TV.

My Worldwide Amateur Radio Friends

About Rob Norman VK5SW.com

Rob Norman, VK5SW became interested in the hobby of Amateur Radio while in high school. Despite severe mental illness at the time, he became fully licensed at the age of 19 and has been an Amateur Radio Operator for over 50 years and although living 100 miles away

from his Australian Bush Block in the Country, he nowadays controls his Solar Powered Amateur Radio Station there remotely via the Internet, although presently the system suffers from a Server problem. His creativity and helpful Amateur Radio Information can be seen on his Website at www.VK5SW.com This Amateur Radio Website includes over 20 Amateur Radio Links which Rob has created. His books which are available in both Amazon Paperback and Kindle versions Worldwide will also inspire You.

Over the last 10 years or so, Rob has created over 150 videos and music slideshows which cover a wide range of topics but are all designed to uplift You. These are best viewed on Your Smart TV by going to ' You tube ' and searching ' VK5SW.' The World is in turmoil, but Amateur Radio is always a constant source of pleasure and his You tube videos and music slideshows may enable You to feel good too.